Woolbur

By Leslie Helakoski

Pictures by Lee Harper

HARPERCOLLINSPUBLISHERS

To my maa, Sally Hébert, for honoring all.
—L. Helakoski

To Beatrice Clauer Harper.
—L. Harper

"**W**oolbur had a little trouble with the herd today," said Maa.

"What happened?" asked Paa.

"I don't want to stand still with the sheep," said Woolbur. "I ran with the dogs instead."

"But those dogs are half wild!" said Paa.

"I know," said Woolbur. "Isn't it great?"

"They'll run circles around you!" said Maa.

"I know," said Woolbur. "Isn't it great?"

"Don't worry," said Grandpaa.

But Maa and Paa pulled on their wool all night long.

"Woolbur had a little trouble in the shearing barn today," said Maa.

"What happened?" asked Paa.

"I don't want to shear my wool," said Woolbur. "Being woolly feels nice."

"But it's springtime!" said Paa.
"I know," said Woolbur.
"Isn't it great?"
"Your wool is so long!" said Maa.
"I know," said Woolbur.
"Isn't it great?"

"Don't worry," said Grandpaa.

But Maa and Paa pulled on their wool all night long.

"Woolbur had a little trouble carding wool today," said Maa.
"What happened?" asked Paa.

"I carded my own wool," said Woolbur. "No more tangles."

"But sheep don't card wool on their bodies!" said Paa.
"I know," said Woolbur. "Isn't it great?"

"You look so different!" said Maa.
"I know," said Woolbur. "Isn't it great?"

"Don't worry," said Grandpaa.

But Maa and Paa pulled on their wool all night long.

"Woolbur had a little trouble spinning today," said Maa.

"What happened?" asked Paa.

"I rode around on the spinning wheel," said Woolbur. "It was fun."

"But spinning is not supposed to be fun!" said Paa.

"I know," said Woolbur. "Isn't it great?"

"Your yarn is all loopy!" said Maa.

"I know," said Woolbur. "Isn't it great?"

"Don't worry," said Grandpaa.

But Maa and Paa pulled on their wool all night long.

"Woolbur had a little trouble dyeing wool today," said Maa. "What happened?" asked Paa.

"Instead of dyeing the yarn, I dyed myself,"
 said Woolbur. "I like experimenting."
"You look unbelievable!" said Paa.
"I know," said Woolbur. "Isn't it great?"
"It will never wash out!" said Maa.
"I know," said Woolbur. "Isn't it great?

"Don't worry," said Grandpaa.

But Maa and Paa pulled on their wool all night long.

"Woolbur had a little trouble weaving today," said Maa.

"What happened?" asked Paa.

"I put my head in the loom," said Woolbur. "To weave my forelock."

"But that's not what you were shown!" said Paa.

"It's unheard of!" said Maa.

"I know," said Woolbur. "Isn't it great?"

"Don't worry," said Grandpaa.

But Maa and Paa pulled on their wool all night long.

Finally Maa and Paa took Woolbur aside and said,
"You must follow the flock, dear. It is what we sheep do.

From now on . . .

You will stay with the herd like everyone else.
You will shear wool like everyone else.
You will card wool like everyone else.
You will spin wool like everyone else.
You will dye wool like everyone else.
You will weave wool like everyone else."

"Oh," said Woolbur.

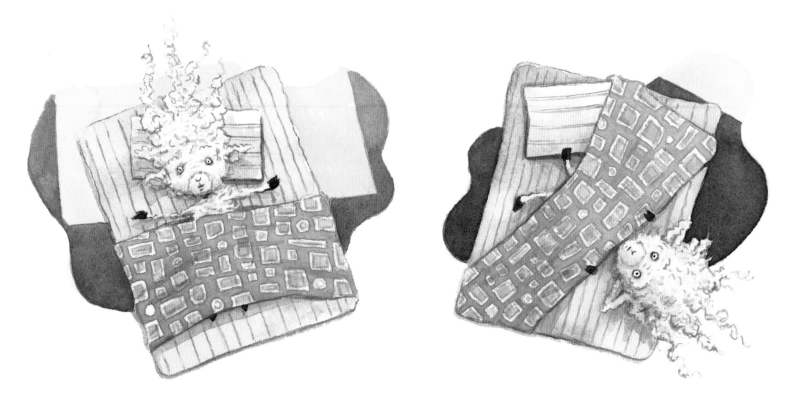

He thought and thought all night long.

And from then on . . .

he taught everyone to run with the dogs,

to let their wool grow,

to card their own wool,

to spin crazy yarn,

to experiment with color,

and to weave their forelocks.

Maa and Paa put their heads in their hooves and sighed.
"Woolbur does not think like we do," said Maa.
"I know," said Paa.
"Now everyone looks like Woolbur and acts like Woolbur," said Maa.
"I know," said Paa. "How will we ever find him?"

"Don't worry," said Grandpaa.